50¢

A Note from Michelle about the Great Pet Project

Hi! I'm Michelle Tanner. I'm eight years old. Do you know what I want more than anything? A pet of my own.

My dad says no. I've just got to change his mind! He says we already have a family pet. (Our dog, Comet.) I love Comet a lot. But I still want a pet that's all mine. Even though Dad says we don't have enough room in our house.

Our house is really big—but lots of people live in it. There's me and my dad. Then there's my two older sisters, D.J. and Stephanie. But that's not all.

My mom died when I was little. So Uncle Jesse moved in to help take care of us. So did Joey Gladstone. He's my dad's friend from college. It's almost like having three dads. But that's still not all!

First Uncle Jesse got married to Becky Donaldson. Then they had twin boys, Nicky and Alex. They're three years old now. And they're so cute.

That's nine people. And our dog, Comet, makes ten. Sure, it gets kind of crazy sometimes. But I wouldn't change it for anything. It's so much fun to live in a full house!

FULL HOUSE™ MICHELLE novels

The Great Pet Project
The Super-Duper Sleepover Party
My Two Best Friends
Lucky, Lucky Day
The Ghost in My Closet
Ballet Surprise

Available from MINSTREL Books

For orders other than by individual consumers, Minstrel Books grants a discount on the purchase of **10 or more** copies of single titles for special markets or premium use. For further details, please write to the Vice-President of Special Markets, Pocket Books, 1230 Avenue of the Americas, New York, NY 10020.

For information on how individual consumers can place orders, please write to Mail Order Department, Paramount Publishing, 200 Old Tappan Road, Old Tappan, NJ 07675.

FULL HOUSE™
Michelle

The Great Pet Project

Jacqueline Carroll

A Parachute Press Book

PUBLISHED BY POCKET BOOKS

New York London Toronto Sydney Tokyo Singapore

The sale of this book without its cover is unauthorized. If you purchased this book without a cover, you should be aware that it was reported to the publisher as "unsold and destroyed." Neither the author nor the publisher has received payment for the sale of this "stripped book."

This book is a work of fiction. Names, characters, places and incidents are products of the author's imagination or are used fictitiously. Any resemblance to actual events or locales or persons, living or dead, is entirely coincidental.

A MINSTREL PAPERBACK *Original*

A Minstrel Book published by
POCKET BOOKS, a division of Simon & Schuster Inc.
1230 Avenue of the Americas, New York, NY 10020

A Parachute Press Book
Copyright © 1995 by Warner Bros. Television

FULL HOUSE, characters, names and all related indicia are trademarks of Warner Bros. Television © 1994.

All rights reserved, including the right to reproduce this book or portions thereof in any form whatsoever. For information address Pocket Books, 1230 Avenue of the Americas, New York, NY 10020

ISBN: 0-671-51905-0

First Minstrel Books printing January 1995

10 9 8 7 6 5 4

A MINSTREL BOOK and colophon are registered trademarks of Simon & Schuster Inc.

Cover photo © 1994 Capital Cities/ABC, Inc. (Craig Sjodin).

Printed in the U.S.A.

The Great Pet Project

Chapter 1

"What did your mom and dad give you for your birthday, Cassie?" Michelle Tanner asked.

Michelle was walking home from school with her best friend, Cassie Wilkins. They were in the third grade together. Cassie had just turned eight years old. Now both of them were the same age.

"They gave me something super-special!" Cassie said. "I'll show you when we get to my house."

"I can't wait!" Michelle said. "I bet you got the purple roller skates with the flashing yellow lights on the wheels. Right?"

"Wrong." Cassie's brown eyes twinkled. "Give up, Michelle. You'll never guess what it is."

Michelle twisted a strand of blond hair around her finger. She thought some more. "I've got it!" she said. "It's the Malibu Monica Doll—the one that comes with her own surfboard."

Cassie shook her head. "Better than that."

"What's better than a doll that can surf in your own bathtub?"

"You'll see!" Cassie laughed and opened the door of her house. The two girls put their book bags in the living room. They said hi to Mrs. Wilkins. Cassie told Michelle to close her eyes. Then she led her into the kitchen.

"Okay," Cassie said. "You can look now."

Michelle opened her eyes. "Oh, wow!" she said.

A little dachshund puppy was sitting inside a bright blue dog-food dish. He had silky brown hair, big brown eyes, and floppy ears.

"You were right!" Michelle cried. "A puppy is a *zillion* times better than Malibu Monica."

The puppy wagged his tail when he saw Cassie. Then he ran to her with a happy bark.

"He's really glad to see you, Cassie," Michelle said. "I bet he missed you while you were at school."

Michelle and Cassie sat down on the floor to play with the puppy. He climbed into Cassie's lap and licked her face.

"Isn't he great?" Cassie said. "He sleeps in a basket next to my bed. And he already follows me all over the place. Watch what he can do."

Cassie rolled a small rubber ball across

the floor. The puppy yipped and chased after it. Then Cassie made a kissing sound and clapped her hands. "Okay. Now bring it back!"

The puppy dashed back to Cassie. He dropped the ball at her feet. He looked very proud of himself.

Michelle laughed. "He's so cute. He's like a fat little hot dog with ears and a tail," she said. "What's his name?"

"I don't know yet," Cassie said. "I'm going through the alphabet, trying to find the perfect one. Right now, I'm on *C*. Maybe Claude. Or Chuck."

"Casper?" Michelle suggested. "Chester?"

"Maybe," Cassie said. "I think I'll try some *D*'s. Danny. Dexter. David. I just don't know." She picked up the ball. "Okay," she said to the puppy. "Go get it!"

The little dog raced after the ball. This time he dropped it in front of Michelle. Then he climbed into her lap and licked her chin. Michelle giggled and petted his silky fur. Then she rolled the ball across the floor. The puppy chased after it again.

"You're really lucky, Cassie," Michelle said. "Your puppy loves you so much. I wish I could have a pet."

"You already do," Cassie said. "Comet, remember?"

"I know," Michelle said. Comet was the Tanner family's golden retriever. "But he isn't only mine. He belongs to all of us."

"Oh, yeah, that's right." Cassie nodded.

Michelle sighed. "I wish I could ask Dad for my very own pet. But I know what he would say." She put on a worried face. She made her voice as deep as she could to sound like her father. "But Michelle, honey. We already have nine people and a dog in the house. Where would we put a new pet?"

Cassie giggled. "That's a good question. Where *would* you put it?"

"I don't know," Michelle said. "But I'd

find someplace." Her house was big, but a lot of people lived in it. There was her father, Danny. There were her two older sisters, D.J. and Stephanie. Her uncle Jesse and his wife, Becky, lived on the third floor. And they had three-year-old twins, Nicky and Alex. Then there was Joey Gladstone, her father's friend from his college days. He lived in the basement. And Comet lived everywhere. It was a very full house.

"You could try to *make* Comet your own special pet," Cassie said.

Michelle frowned. "How?"

"Well, do more things with him," Cassie said.

"You mean like play Frisbee with him every day?"

Cassie nodded. "Teach him some new tricks."

Michelle liked that idea. She could spend more time with Comet. Then maybe they'd become best friends. It would almost be like having a dog of her very own.

"I'll talk to him a lot, too," she said. "And give him hundreds of hugs." She jumped up. "That's a great idea, Cassie. I'm going home and try it right now!"

Chapter 2

Michelle couldn't wait to make Comet her own special pet. She ran up the steps to her house. She flung open the front door. "Comet!" she called. "Guess who's here? It's me—Michelle!"

"Woof!" Comet barked from the kitchen.

Michelle hurried through the living room to the kitchen. Comet sat on the floor, wagging his tail. He had wavy golden hair and friendly dark eyes. When he stood up, he almost reached Michelle's shoulders.

"Hi, Comet!" Michelle said. She wrapped her arms around his neck and squeezed. "Did you miss me today? I missed you. I bet you're starving, aren't you? And I know just what you want. You want a snack."

Michelle went to the cabinet and pulled out a box of Canine Chewies. She took out one of the bone-shaped dog biscuits and held it up in front of Comet. His tail wagged even harder. Michelle dropped a Chewie into his mouth. Comet wolfed it down.

"Come on, Comet," Michelle said. "I want to talk to you about something." She carried the box of Canine Chewies into the living room. Comet followed, wagging his tail.

"Good dog," Michelle said. She sat down on the couch and took out another Chewie. "Now sit."

Comet sat down in front of her. He stared at the Chewie in her hand.

"Listen, Comet," Michelle said. "I know you belong to the whole family. But could you try to be mostly *my* dog? I'll play with you. I'll talk to you. We'll go for long walks together. Won't that be fun?"

Comet kept staring at the second Chewie. Michelle gave it to him. "You'll be my best dog friend. And I'll be your best human friend. Okay, Comet? Do you want to shake on it?"

Michelle held out her hand. Comet raised a paw and gently placed it on her palm. "Good dog!" she said. She shook his paw and grinned. "Now you're my special pet."

Just then the front door opened. Joey came in. Comet barked happily and bounded over to him.

"Hi, Michelle," Joey said. "Hey, Comet!" He rubbed the dog's head. "Glad to see me? Good, slap me five!"

Joey held his palm up. Comet hit it with his paw.

Michelle was surprised. "When did he learn how to do a high five?" she asked.

"Oh, I taught him just a few days ago," Joey said.

Suddenly Michelle remembered that *she* was going to teach Comet some new tricks. "Come here, Comet!" she said.

But the dog wouldn't come. He kept prancing around Joey's feet. Then the front door opened again. Michelle's father, Danny, and D.J., her older sister, came in. Comet trotted over to them with another happy bark.

"Come on, Comet!" Michelle said. "I'll teach you to dance. Want to learn to hip hop?"

But Comet just ignored her. He began to run circles around Danny.

"I'm not sure Comet's ready to hip hop, honey," Danny said to Michelle. "You know the saying."

"What saying?"

"You can't teach an old dog new tricks," D.J. said.

"But Comet's not old. He's only eight," Michelle said.

"Dogs age faster than people," her dad said. "Comet would be older than I am if he were human."

Michelle frowned. Maybe Comet was old. But Joey had taught him to do a high five. He *could* learn new tricks. And she could teach him. "Comet, come!" she called.

At that moment Stephanie came in the door. Comet jumped up, putting his paws on her shoulders, and almost knocked her down.

Stephanie laughed. "Whoa, Comet! I've only been gone a few hours."

"Comet!" Michelle said. "Remember what we talked about? Remember the two Chewies I gave you? You're supposed to be my best friend."

Comet didn't seem to hear her. He

jumped up on Joey and tried to lick his face.

Michelle slumped back against the couch. This wasn't going to work. Comet was supposed to be her special dog friend. But he had already forgotten their deal. Michelle knew it wasn't Comet's fault. He probably hadn't even understood.

"Hey, Michelle," Danny said. "Why do you look so sad?" He sat down next to her on the couch.

"I need to ask you something, Dad."

"Sure, honey. Go ahead," Danny said.

Michelle took a deep breath. She crossed her fingers. "Can I have a pet of my own?"

Chapter 3

"A pet?" Danny looked at Comet. "But we already have one."

"That's right," Michelle said. "*We* have one. Comet belongs to the whole family."

"That makes him your pet too," Joey said.

"But I want my very own pet. Like Cassie," Michelle said. "She just got a new puppy."

"Oh, *I* get it." Stephanie said. "It's just like when Cassie got that new bike. You know, the one with the pink and white streamers on the handlebars? You wanted one just like it."

"I did not," Michelle said. "I wanted *yellow* and white streamers. Besides, this is different. I've been wanting my own pet for a long time. Dexter just made me want one more."

Danny looked puzzled. "Who's Dexter?"

"It's one of the names Cassie might call her puppy," Michelle said. "You should see him, Dad. He comes when she calls him. And she already taught him to fetch. He's all hers. I want a pet that's all mine. Comet's all *ours.*"

Danny started to straighten the magazines on the coffee table into a neat pile. He was a neat-freak. And Michelle could always tell when he was nervous. He got even neater!

"But Michelle, honey, we already have nine people and a dog in the house," Danny said. "Where would we put a new pet?"

"I knew you were going to say that," Michelle said. "But that's not what you said when Nicky and Alex were born. Then you said 'the more, the merrier.' "

Stephanie laughed. "You did, Dad. And you bought Uncle Jesse all those blue bubblegum cigars to hand out."

"Yeah, Dad," D.J. said. "Besides, every kid wants a pet. I know I did."

"True," Joey said. "I wanted a monkey."

"I wanted a kitten," Stephanie said. "But all I got was a hermit crab."

Danny found a dustcloth. He started dusting the table.

D.J. laughed. "Well, I wanted a pony. Remember, Dad?"

Danny dusted even faster. "Oh, boy, I sure do!"

Michelle could tell that the idea of a great big pet made her father *really* nervous. "Don't worry, Dad," she said. "I don't want a pony."

"Well, that's a relief!" Danny tossed down the dustcloth and looked at his watch. "Hey, look at the time! It's our night to cook, Joey. D.J., your turn to make the salad. Stephanie, don't forget to set the table. Come on, everybody, let's get to work!"

It was Michelle's night to clear the table after dinner. So she didn't follow the others into the kitchen. She stayed on the couch and thought.

Her dad had changed the subject very fast. He probably hoped she'd forget all about wanting a pet of her own. But she wouldn't.

And she wasn't going to let her dad forget it, either.

Michelle didn't talk much at dinner that night. She just kept thinking. And thinking. How was she going to talk her father into letting her have a pet? There just had to be a way!

"Hey, guess what, you guys?" Uncle Jesse said. He reached for a fried-chicken leg. "We got a new job today." Jesse played the guitar in a band. "There's a big concert in the park Sunday night. We're doing the opening and closing numbers."

I could refuse to eat until he says yes, Michelle thought. But what about Friday night? That was pizza night. She couldn't say no to pizza!

"I got a new job too," Joey said. "At Club Chuckle." Joey was a comedian. "Now all I have to do is come up with some good jokes." He thought a minute. "How about this one? My neighbor is so rich, his dog has its own car. And he built a special place to keep it—a barking lot. Get it? A *barking* lot!"

"I thought you wanted to come up with some *good* jokes," Stephanie teased.

Michelle drank some milk. She was still trying to figure out how to get a pet. I could look real sad and cry a lot, she thought.

But she'd tried that once—when she was

five and wanted a skateboard. It didn't work. Her dad just gave her a big box of tissues to dry her tears.

"The twins and I had a great time this afternoon," Becky said. "We went to the zoo."

"We saw tigers," Alex said.

"And effalunts," Nicky added.

"Elephants, Nicky," Becky corrected him. "Elephants."

Nicky nodded. "Big ones," he said. He stretched his hand way up over his head to show how big.

"Michelle?" Becky said. "How was your day? Did anything special happen?"

"Not to me," Michelle said. "But Cassie got a puppy. A dachshund. He's so cute!"

Stephanie rolled her eyes. "Here we go again!"

"What do you mean?" Becky asked.

"Michelle wants a new pet," Stephanie told her.

"Really? What kind?" Jesse asked.

"I don't know," Michelle said. "But I want it to be my very own."

"That makes sense." Jesse said. "Why don't you get a bird? Maybe a parrot. You could teach it to talk."

"I always wanted a snake when I was a kid," Joey said.

"I thought you wanted a monkey," Stephanie said.

"I did. I wanted a snake too." Joey held his arms out wide. "A big boa constrictor!"

D.J. looked at Michelle. "If you bring a snake into this house, I'm outta here!"

"I still say a bird's the best," Jesse said.

"No," Alex said. "A tiger."

"An effalunt," Nicky said. "Get an effalunt!"

"No way." Stephanie shook her head. "I'm not sharing my room with an effalunt."

Michelle giggled. Everybody laughed.

Then Danny tapped his glass with a fork. He cleared his throat and smiled.

"You've all given Michelle some good ideas," he said. "But isn't everybody forgetting something?"

"Oh, no, Michelle thought. He was going to say there wasn't enough room again.

"What have we forgotten?" Joey asked.

"One word," Danny said, looking serious. "Responsibility."

Michelle hadn't even thought of *that.*

"Taking care of a pet—your very own pet—is a big responsibility," Danny said.

"Right," Stephanie said. "Especially if it's an elephant."

"I'm not kidding." Danny sounded serious. "Take Comet, for example."

Comet's ears perked up when he heard his name. Danny scratched him on the head.

"Comet needs to be fed and walked every day," he said. "He has to be brushed and washed. Sometimes he makes a big mess. And somebody has to clean it up.

What if he gets sick or hurt? Somebody has to take him to the vet."

"I could do all of that," Michelle said. "Except take him to the vet. Besides, I didn't say I wanted a dog."

"I know," Danny said. "But you're only eight years old, honey. I'm just not sure you're ready for your own pet. No matter what it is."

"But I am. I know I am!" Suddenly Michelle had an idea. "Dad? What if I *prove* I'm responsible enough? Then could I have my own pet?"

"I guess I'd have to see." Danny frowned. "But how are you going to prove it?"

"I don't know," Michelle admitted. "But I'll think of something!"

Chapter 4

Michelle told Cassie about her plan at school the next day.

"So all you have to do is prove you're responsible, right?" Cassie asked. "Then you can have your own pet?"

"Not exactly," Michelle said. "Dad said he'd have to see."

"Uh-oh," Cassie said. "I hate it when my mom and dad say 'we'll see.' It almost always means *no.*"

"Dad too," Michelle said. "But I'm still going to try."

"How will you prove you can do it?"

Cassie asked. "Are you going to take care of Comet all by yourself?"

Michelle shook her head. "Comet doesn't listen to me. Not the way Dexter listens to you."

"Who's Dexter?"

"Your puppy, remember?" Michelle said. "Or did you decide to call him David?"

Cassie shook her head. "I couldn't find any *D* names I really liked. I'm on the *P*'s now. Pancho. Pete. Paul."

"How about Pasta?" Michelle said. "He's going to be long and squiggly, like macaroni."

"Attention, class!" Mrs. Wexley called out. "Everyone quiet down for a minute. I have an announcement."

Everyone got quiet. The teacher walked over to the Nature Corner. She put her hand on top of a big wire cage and said, "Lee's parents have given him permission to take Boris and Natasha home with him this weekend. Thank you, Lee. Take good care of your guests."

Boris and Natasha were two white mice. They spent their weekdays in the classroom. One of the students always took them home on the weekends.

Michelle stared at the mouse house. "That's it!" she cried.

"What's it?" Cassie asked.

"I just thought of a way to prove how responsible I am," she said. "I'll take Boris and Natasha home this weekend. Dad will see how well I take care of them. Then he'll have to give in!"

Cassie looked puzzled. "But Lee's taking them home."

"Not if I can talk him out of it," Michelle said.

"How are you going to do that?"

Michelle frowned. "That's a good question."

At last it was lunchtime. The class lined up and went to the cafeteria. Now's my chance to talk to Lee! Michelle thought.

She sat down right across from him at a table.

Michelle opened her lunch box. "Lee, I have a problem," she said. "And I need your help."

Lee smiled. "Can I have your pickle?" he asked.

"Sure." Michelle watched as Lee ate the pickle in three bites. "It's like this," she said. "I want to get my own pet. Maybe a cat. Or a rabbit. I can't decide."

"Get a tarantula," Lee said. "They're really cool."

Yuck! Michelle thought. She didn't like spiders. Especially big hairy spiders. She shivered just thinking about them.

"Well, anyway," she said. "My dad doesn't think I'm responsible enough to have my own pet. But just think. What if I took Boris and Natasha home this weekend? I could show my dad how responsible I am."

"But I'm taking them," Lee said. "I already told Flat Top."

"Who's Flat Top?"

"My pet turtle."

"But you could take them next week," Michelle said. "I just know Flat Top would understand."

"I have a question," Lee said.

"What?"

"Are you going to eat the other half of your sandwich?" he asked.

Michelle looked at the sandwich her dad had made that morning. It was stuffed with roast turkey, thin slices of tomato, and crispy lettuce.

Then she looked at Lee's sandwich. Peanut butter, as usual. And not even any jelly.

That's it! Michelle thought. Then she grinned at Lee.

"I'm full!" she said. "You can have it. Here." Michelle handed him the sandwich. "My dad makes the greatest lunches." She reached into her lunch box and pulled out some cookies. "And the best desserts."

Lee's eyes lit up. "Chocolate chip?"

"Yeah. Homemade," Michelle said. "Here. Have one."

"Thanks." Lee took a bite of the cookie.

"Listen, Lee. I'll make a deal with you," Michelle said. "You let me have Boris and Natasha this weekend. And I'll trade lunches with you for the rest of the week. Please, Lee? Is it a deal?"

Lee swallowed. "Does that include desserts?"

Michelle nodded.

"Deal," Lee said, smiling. Then he finished the cookie.

Michelle was very nervous when she got home that afternoon.

She had gotten Lee to go along with her plan. And Mrs. Wexley had agreed to let her bring Boris and Natasha home. Lee would take them next weekend.

But would her dad say okay?

She stuck the permission slip for the mice on the refrigerator door. Mrs. Wexley said her father had to sign it before she could bring the mice home.

He has to sign it, Michelle thought. He just *has* to!

Danny didn't notice the slip of paper until dinner was over. He started to put the milk away. Then suddenly he stopped.

"What's this?" he asked. He peered at the refrigerator door and began to read: "I, the parent/guardian of blank, give my permission for my daughter/son to bring Boris and Natasha home for the weekend."

"Boris and Natasha?" Becky said. "Aren't they those two cartoon characters?"

Michelle nodded. "But the Boris and Natasha I want to bring home are mice."

"Mice?" Danny almost dropped the milk carton. "Did you say mice?"

"Sure. Don't you remember, Dad?" Michelle said. "You met them at Open School Night."

"Oh, *that* Boris and Natasha!" Danny put away the milk and looked at Michelle. "You want to bring two rodents home for the weekend?"

"They're not rodents. They're mice," Michelle said.

"Same thing, Michelle," Stephanie said.

"Oh. Well, anyway, the whole class takes care of them on school days," Michelle said. "But somebody has to take them home on the weekends."

"Two mice with red eyes and twitchy pink noses?" Danny asked. "And you volunteered to bring them home?"

Danny started stacking the empty plates. Michelle could tell he was nervous about having mice in the house. But she knew there was nothing to worry about.

"Remember what you told me, Dad?" Michelle asked. "You said I had to prove

I was responsible enough to take care of a pet. Then maybe I could have my own."

"She's right, Dad," D.J. told him. "That's what you said. We all heard you."

"I think it's a great idea," Becky said. "And Nicky and Alex will love them."

"Come on, Danny. You're not afraid of two little mice, are you?" Jesse teased.

Danny sighed. "I'm just not crazy about the idea of having mice around, that's all."

"They live in their own mouse house," Michelle said. "It's a big wire cage. And you won't have to clean it. That's my job."

"Well . . ." Danny looked around the table. "What does everybody else think? Stephanie, what about you? Do you mind having two mice for roommates?"

"Do they snore?" Stephanie joked.

"They'll be as quiet as mice. I promise," Michelle said. She looked at her father. "Please?"

Just then the phone rang. Joey answered it. "Tanner Mouse Motel!" he said. "Hold on. Michelle, it's Mickey and Minnie. They want to know if they can come play with Boris and Natasha this weekend. Just kidding. It's Cassie."

Michelle laughed and took the phone. "Hello?"

"What did your dad say?" Cassie asked. "Do you get to take Boris and Natasha home?"

Michelle looked at Danny. "What do you say, Dad?"

"Okay, honey," Danny said. "Bring on the mice."

Michelle grinned. "He says yes!"

Chapter 5

At last! It was Friday afternoon. Danny drove Michelle, Boris, and Natasha home from school.

"Here we are, guys!" Michelle said. She set the big wire cage inside the front door. "Welcome to the Tanner house!"

Comet heard Michelle's voice and dashed in from the kitchen. Then he saw the cage. His ears perked up and his tail wagged. He ran over and began to sniff the mouse house.

Boris jumped onto the exercise wheel and started running. Natasha stood up on her hind legs and sniffed the air.

Comet took a step back. Then he sat down and barked.

The barking scared the mice. Boris ran faster on the wheel. Natasha dropped onto all fours and froze.

"Be nice, Comet," Michelle said. "You're scaring our guests." She patted the dog on the head. Then she shouted, "Hey, everybody! The mice are here."

"Boris! Tasha!" The twins ran down the stairs. Joey came in from the kitchen. Within seconds the cage was surrounded. Michelle was glad the mice were used to lots of people.

Comet had stopped barking. So now Boris stopped running so fast on the wheel. Natasha climbed on top of a blue plastic cube. She stared out at Joey.

"Boris, your eyes are so red," Joey said. "Didn't you get enough sleep?"

Michelle laughed. "That's Natasha, Joey."

Danny peered into the cage. "How can you tell them apart?" he asked.

Michelle pointed to the mouse on the wheel. "See how thick his tail is where it connects to his body? That means he's a he."

"Well, well!" Danny said. "You learn something new every day, don't you?"

"Boris likes to go round and round," Nicky said.

Alex poked his finger into the cage. Natasha sniffed it. "Can Tasha come out and play?" Alex asked.

Michelle really wanted to say yes. But her father looked a little worried. I better give Dad time to get used to them, Michelle thought.

"Not right now, Alex," she said. "I'm going to take Boris and Natasha upstairs. I want to show them their room. Why don't you guys play with Comet for a while? I think he's jealous of all the attention the mice are getting."

Comet whined when he heard his name. The twins started petting him. Danny looked relieved that the mice were staying in the cage.

Michelle carried the mouse house upstairs. She set it on top of her dresser. Then she pulled the desk chair over and sat down.

"Listen," she said to the mice. "I know this house is a little crazy sometimes. But you'll get used to it. Here's the important thing. We've got two days to show my dad that I'm a responsible person. And you've got to help me, okay?"

Boris was drinking from the water bottle. Natasha was still perched on the blue cube.

"Okay," Michelle said. "So don't do anything dumb."

Boris kept drinking. Natasha climbed off the cube and onto the exercise wheel. It squeaked as she ran around and around.

Michelle kept watching them. She wondered what she could do next. She needed a way to show her father how well she could take care of her pets. She got up and looked out the window. The mailman was coming up the front walk.

"Hey, let's get the mail," Michelle said to the mice. She picked up the cage and lugged it back downstairs.

Danny watched her drag the cage through the living room. "What's up?" he asked.

"We're getting the mail," Michelle said.

"Aha. Are Boris and Natasha expecting a letter?"

"Very funny, Dad," Michelle said. "I just didn't want to leave them all by themselves. They're my responsibility, you know."

Michelle got the mail. It was mostly bills and junk mail. Then she carried the cage back upstairs.

"Now what?" she asked the mice. "I know! I'll clean your house. But first I'll have to get you out of the way. Where can I put you?" She looked around the room. "How about the dresser drawer?"

Michelle pulled open the bottom drawer of the dresser. Then she opened the door of the mouse cage. She put her hand inside, palm up. Natasha sniffed it, then climbed on.

Michelle slowly pulled her hand out of the cage. She rubbed the soft white fur on Natasha's head with her finger. Then she gently put the mouse on top of a yellow sweater in the drawer.

Next Michelle took Boris out of the cage. She stroked his head and put him down next to Natasha. Then she closed the drawer. But she left it open a little so the mice could breathe.

"Now, you stay there and take a nap," Michelle said. "And I'll clean your house."

It took Michelle a half hour to clean the mouse house. She dumped the old wood shavings into a garbage bag. She washed the cage. Then she poured in new shavings from a bag she'd brought home from school.

Let's see, thought Michelle. What next?

She threw away Boris and Natasha's old food. She put new pellets into their food dish. She filled the water dispenser with fresh water. Then she went to get the mice.

Natasha was still sitting on top of the yellow sweater.

"Hello, sweetie," Michelle said. She grinned at the little white mouse. "Where's Boris?"

Natasha just twitched her nose.

Michelle's smile disappeared. "Boris? . . . Boris! Where are you?"

Boris was nowhere in sight!

Chapter 6

♡ Calm down! Michelle told herself. I'm sure he's here somewhere. . . .

But her heart pounded with fear.

She put Natasha back in the cage and shut the door. Then she started looking for Boris.

He must be under something, she thought. Carefully she lifted out the yellow sweater. She felt it gently before she put it on the floor. No Boris.

She took out a sweatshirt. Still no Boris. Could he have dug all the way down to the bottom of the drawer?

Soon there was a pile of sweaters and sweatshirts on the floor. Michelle looked inside. The drawer was empty. No clothes. No mouse, either.

Just then the door opened. Michelle jumped. Danny stuck his head inside. "Michelle, time to set the table," he said.

"Okay, Dad." Michelle tried to sound calm.

"What are you doing?" he asked. "Cleaning out the dresser?"

"Um. Sort of," Michelle said. She looked all around. Suddenly she noticed a sock that Stephanie had left by her bed. A pink sock. A pink, wiggling sock. Boris! He must have climbed out of the drawer and found a new nest.

Oh, no! Michelle thought. She couldn't let her father see that one of the mice was loose!

Michelle jumped up and ran to the door. She gave Danny a kiss. "Thanks for letting me bring the mice home, Dad. I'll be down in just a second to set the table. See you!"

She waited till her dad left. Then she slammed the door. "That was close!"

She raced across the room and picked up the pink sock. Boris peeked out and twitched his whiskers.

Michelle put Boris back in the cage and shut the wire door. "Didn't I tell you not to do anything dumb?"

Boris dashed quickly to the food dish and started nibbling.

Michelle took the mouse house with her when she went downstairs to set the table. Danny didn't want it in the kitchen. So Michelle put it on the table in the living room. But she kept getting up to check on them. And her pizza got cold.

After dinner Michelle and the mice watched television.

After that the mouse house sat on the bathroom floor while Michelle took a bath.

After *that* she took them up to her room

and put them on top of the dresser. She gave them fresh water and fresh food again. Then she sat and watched them some more.

Stephanie came in and got ready for bed. She saw her sister staring at the mice. "Michelle, all those mice are doing is chewing," she said. "Aren't you getting bored just looking at them?"

"A little," Michelle admitted. "But I have to show Dad how responsible I am."

"Dad can't even see you right now," Stephanie said. "Lighten up, okay? You don't have to keep your eye on them every single second. Besides, I have to get up early. Time to turn off the light and go to bed."

Michelle yawned. She was getting sleepy. Maybe Stephanie was right. After all, nobody watched the mice when they were at school at night. "Good night, Natasha," she whispered. "Good night, Boris. Sleep tight."

* * *

After breakfast on Saturday morning Michelle was bored. She was so bored that even doing a little homework would be fun. But Mrs. Wexley didn't give homework on the weekends.

Boris and Natasha were spinning on their wheel. At least the mice had something to do. Now Michelle needed something to do.

Suddenly the phone rang. "I'll get it!" she called out. She ran to the phone in the upstairs hall. She picked up the receiver on the third ring. "Hello."

"Hi, Michelle, it's Cassie. I've got a new leash and collar for my puppy. I'm going to take him for a walk. Want to come?"

"Definitely!" Michelle said. "Let me check with Dad." Michelle set down the phone. She found Danny in the kitchen, putting a dish in the oven.

"Hey, Dad," Michelle said. "Is it okay if I go with Cassie to walk her dog?"

"Sure, honey." Danny took off his

apron and folded it neatly. "But can you be home for lunch? I've got a new taco casserole I want to try out on everybody."

Michelle hurried back to the phone. "I'll meet you halfway in ten minutes," she told Cassie.

Michelle jumped into her clothes. She quickly brushed her hair into a ponytail. Then she tied her sneakers as fast as she could.

She was about to run out the door. But she stopped in her tracks and looked back at the mouse house. She sighed. Then she grabbed the cage and hurried outside.

Michelle met Cassie and her puppy halfway up the block. Cassie stared in surprise at the cage. "How come you brought Boris and Natasha?"

"I thought they'd like the fresh air," Michelle said. "Besides, I didn't want to run off and leave them all alone. Dad might say I wasn't being responsible."

The puppy jumped up and sniffed at the

cage. Michelle patted him on the head. "Have you named him yet?" she asked.

Cassie shook her head. "Nope. I'm on the *R*'s now. What do you think of Rex?"

"I'm not sure," Michelle said. "He doesn't look like a Rex. How about Ralph? Or Rudy?"

Cassie sighed. "I can't make up my mind," she said. "But I better think of something or I'll run out of letters." She tugged on the leash. "Okay," she said to the puppy. "Let's take a walk."

The walk was fun—for Cassie and Rex, Ralph, or Rudy. The puppy sniffed at everything. He wagged his tail at everybody who stopped to pet him.

Michelle was having fun, but she was getting tired. The mouse house got heavier the farther they walked. Her right arm started to ache. So she switched the cage to her left hand.

Pretty soon both arms were aching. She had to change the cage from hand to hand every two minutes. And it hurt when the metal cage banged against her leg.

Finally Cassie and Michelle were back in front of Michelle's house.

"I have to go see my grandmother this afternoon," said Cassie. "But maybe we could get together tomorrow."

"Uh, sure," said Michelle. "That would be fun." All she could think about was going inside to rest!

At home Michelle carried the mouse house into the living room. "That's the last time I'm taking you guys for a walk," she said to the mice. She put their cage down on the coffee table. "Want to watch some cartoons?"

Michelle turned on the TV. Then she flopped down on the couch. Boris and Natasha played on the exercise wheel.

At lunch Michelle left the table only twice to check on the mice. At dinner she left the table only once.

When Michelle went to bed, she put the

cage on top of her dresser. Just as she was about to fall asleep, the wheel started squeaking. Michelle turned on her light and saw that Natasha was running on the exercise wheel. So Michelle put the mouse house out in the hall. She could still hear the squeaking when she got back into bed. So she got up and shut the bedroom door.

Michelle woke up on Sunday morning. She got out of bed and opened the door.

Suddenly she gasped.

The mouse cage was split open.

And standing in the hall were two white mice. But not the little white mice she'd brought home from school. These mice were as big as Comet!

Chapter 7

"Boris! Natasha!" Michelle said. "You've grown!"

The gigantic mice wiggled their whiskers at her.

"Hey, I can take you for a walk now," Michelle said. "Come on. Let's go downstairs and get the leashes."

Like magic, the three of them were out on the sidewalk. It was fun to walk the huge mice on their leashes. They sniffed at everything. Everybody wanted to stop and pet them. And the mice just wagged their tails.

Tweet! A police officer stopped traffic to let Michelle and her pets cross the street. A crowd gathered to watch.

"What beautiful mice!" one lady exclaimed.

"And they're so well behaved!" said her husband. He smiled at Michelle. "You must be a *responsible* young lady."

Michelle felt very proud.

But the giant mice weren't so well behaved when they got home. They went right for the kitchen. They opened the cabinets and started pulling out boxes of food. Cereal, flour, cake mixes, and cookies spilled onto the floor. Soon the mess grew to the size of a mountain. It almost touched the ceiling.

Suddenly the kitchen door opened. It was her father! Danny looked horrified as a mound of Canine Chewies tumbled down on him.

"Boris! Natasha! Stop it!" Michelle cried. "Stop!"

And then she opened her eyes.

She was still in bed. It had only been a dream.

Michelle hopped out of bed and opened the door. The mouse house was right where she left it the night before. Boris was drinking and Natasha was eating. Both of them were tiny.

"Morning, mice," Michelle said. She knelt down next to the cage. "You look happy. You didn't mind sleeping in the hall, did you? Good. I think I'll put you out here tonight, too. I guess Stephanie was right. I *don't* have to keep my eye on you every second."

Michelle picked up the mouse house and took it into her room. She set the cage on the floor next to her bed. Then she brushed her teeth and went downstairs for pancakes.

The phone rang. "It's for you, Michelle," Danny said. "Cassie."

"Hi," Michelle said. "You won't believe the dream I had."

"Tell me later," Cassie said. "On the Ferris wheel."

"The Ferris wheel?"

"Yeah. There's a carnival in the park at the end of our block," Cassie said. "My dad said he'll take us. Want to come?"

"Do I ever! Hold on," Michelle said. "Dad, can I go to the carnival with Cassie? Her dad's going to take us."

"Sure, honey. Sounds like fun."

"I can come," Michelle said into the phone.

"Great," Cassie said. "We'll pick you up in fifteen minutes. See you."

Michelle hung up. "I have to hurry," she said. "Cassie's coming by in fifteen minutes."

"What about the mice?" Stephanie asked.

"Oh, no!" Michelle said. "I can't take mice to a carnival!"

"I know, Michelle," Stephanie said. "I was kidding."

"Is it okay if I leave them here, Dad?" Michelle asked. "Don't worry. You won't have to do a thing. I'll give them fresh food and water before I go."

"It's fine, Michelle," Danny said. He gave her some spending money. "Don't eat too much cotton candy."

"Thanks, Dad." She gave him a kiss and hurried upstairs.

She got dressed and brushed her hair. Then she gave the mice fresh water. They still had plenty of food. But maybe they'd like a treat, she thought. She ran back downstairs for a piece of lettuce. Then she ran up to her room and tossed the lettuce in the cage.

She looked at her watch. She had to go. "I'll clean your house when I get home," she said to the mice. Then she quickly closed the cage door. "See you later!"

Michelle, Cassie, and Mr. Wilkins drove

to the carnival. Then they stood in line to ride the Ferris wheel.

"Look who's in front of us," Cassie said.

It was Lee, the boy Michelle had traded lunches with so she could take home the mice. He was with his mother.

"Hi," Michelle said. "Want to ride with Cassie and me?"

"Sure," Lee said. "How are Boris and Natasha?"

"They're fine." Michelle looked up at the Ferris wheel. "I bet they'd love a ride on this."

"Oh, I forgot to tell you, Michelle," Cassie said. "I finally named my puppy!"

"Great! What?" Michelle asked. "Vinny? Waldo?"

Cassie shook her head.

"Well, what is it? Tell me."

"Okay."

"Okay," Michelle said. "Tell me."

Cassie laughed. *"Okay,"* she said. "That's his name. Every time I called him, I said,

'Okay, come here!' Or 'Okay, bring the ball back!' So I finally decided to name him *Okay.* Do you like it?"

Michelle giggled. "It's *okay!"*

Then it was their turn on the Ferris wheel. The giant wheel took Michelle, Cassie, and Lee high above the carnival. Nobody talked. They just screamed at the top of their lungs!

The three friends rode the Ferris wheel two more times. Next they rode the Whip until they were dizzy. After that they threw darts at balloons and softballs at milk bottles. Then they ate two hot dogs apiece. But they still had room for some cotton candy.

"I wish I could stay here all day," Michelle said. "But I have to go home and check the mice." She sighed. "I'm sure they're not doing anything exciting. Mice are kind of boring."

"I think they're cool," Lee said. He pulled off a glob of pink cotton candy and stuffed it in his mouth. "I can't wait to take Boris and Natasha home. I'm going to teach them how to jump through a hoop."

Michelle frowned. "Can mice really learn to do that?"

"Sure," Lee said. "I read a book about keeping mice as pets."

"Michelle," Cassie said. "Maybe you should teach Boris and Natasha how to do a trick. That would show your dad how good you are with animals."

"That's right," Michelle said. "And he might say yes when I ask for my own pet." She frowned again. "But I don't know how to teach mice anything."

"I do," Lee said. "I could come home with you and show you how. We can bend a wire hanger into a hoop."

"We're not going to light it on fire, are we?" Michelle asked. "Like in a circus?"

Lee grinned. "No, but that would really be cool!"

Lee got permission to go to Michelle's.

Then Cassie's dad drove the three kids to the Tanner house.

"I can't wait to see Boris and Natasha jump through a hoop," Michelle said. She opened the front door for her friends. "Come on. They're in my room."

Upstairs, Michelle went to the closet for a hanger. Lee and Cassie knelt down by the mouse house on the floor.

"Hey, the door's open," Lee said.

Michelle spun around. "What?"

Lee pointed to the side of the cage. He was right. The little door was partway open.

"But . . ." Michelle gulped. "Are the mice still inside?" She crossed her fingers.

"I see Boris," Cassie said. "His tail's poking out from under that piece of lettuce."

Michelle kept her fingers crossed and walked over to the cage. "What about Natasha?"

"Maybe she buried herself under the

wood shavings," Lee said. "Mice like to do that." He stuck his hand in the mouse house and felt all around. Then he shook his head.

Cassie felt around the cage too. But she didn't find Natasha either.

"Let me try," Michelle said. "She has to be here. She just has to be!"

Michelle searched all over the bottom of the cage. Then she took out everything: the exercise wheel, the cube, the ladder, and the food dish. She felt under the shavings again. But it was no use.

Natasha was gone.

Chapter 8

"I'm in trouble now," Michelle said. She and her friends stared into the mouse house. "*Big* trouble."

"How could Natasha have gotten out?" Cassie asked.

"Simple," Lee said. "The door probably wasn't shut tight."

Michelle tried to think. She'd been in a hurry to get ready for the carnival. She'd given the mice fresh water and a piece of lettuce. And she'd closed the door tight. Hadn't she?

"Or maybe somebody took her out," Cassie said.

"The twins!" Michelle cried. "They love the mice. I bet they did it. Come on!"

Michelle raced up to the third floor of her house. "Nicky! Alex!" she called. Cassie and Lee were right behind her.

Becky opened the door. "What's going on?"

"Natasha's not in the cage," Michelle said breathlessly. "Do Nicky and Alex have her?" She crossed her fingers again. "Please say they have her!"

But Becky frowned and shook her head. "Gee, I don't think so, Michelle. We went to the park and then to the mall. We only got back a minute ago."

Just then the twins came running to the door.

"Nicky, Alex!" Michelle said. "Do you know where Natasha is?"

"In the mouse house," Alex said. Nicky nodded.

"She *was* in the mouse house," Michelle said. "But she's not now. Did you take her out to play with her before you went to the park and the mall?"

Both boys shook their heads.

"You can tell me," Michelle said. "I won't be mad. I promise."

The twins shook their heads again. Nicky crossed his heart. Alex crossed his stomach.

They didn't take her, Michelle thought. That means it's my fault. I didn't close the cage door tight enough!

"We have to find her," Michelle said. "She's probably scared to death. And I'm in big trouble if Dad finds out she's missing."

"We'll go on a mouse hunt. Everyone can help," Cassie said.

"Good idea," Becky said. "Lee, why don't you stay up here with the boys and me? We'll check out this floor. Michelle, you and Cassie search the second floor."

"Thanks, Becky," Michelle said.

Cassie grabbed Michelle by the arm.

"Come on. Let's look in your room. I bet that's where we'll find her."

Michelle and Cassie ran into her room. "Look in all the socks," Michelle said. "Boris got into one the day I brought him home. Maybe Natasha likes them too."

Cassie looked through socks and under the beds. Michelle dug deep into the closet. She stuck her hands in every sneaker and boot. Then she tossed each empty one out.

"Hey! Watch out!" Stephanie dodged a black high-top as she came into the room. Then she looked around in surprise and said, "My bed. My shoes. What are you guys doing?"

Michelle backed out of the closet. "Looking for Natasha."

"Natasha? You mean . . ."

Michelle nodded. "She's missing."

"Poor thing," Stephanie said. "Wow, Michelle. If Dad finds out about this—"

"I know!" Michelle cried. "I'm in big trouble!"

"Okay," Stephanie said. "Tell me where to look."

"Thanks, Steph," Michelle said. "Try the dresser drawers."

Stephanie, Cassie, and Michelle turned the room upside down. They were turning it upside down again when D.J. appeared in the doorway.

"Whoa!" D.J. looked at the mess and shook her head. "What's happening?"

"Natasha's missing," Michelle said.

"Natasha the mouse?"

"How many Natashas do you know?" Stephanie asked.

"Wow, Michelle," D.J. said. "If Dad finds out—"

"Please don't say it!" Michelle cried. "I already know."

"Sorry, Michelle," D.J. said. "I'll go look in my room."

"Be sure to check the socks," Cassie told her.

"And walk carefully!" Michelle added. She didn't want somebody to step on the mouse.

They put Michelle's room back together. Then the group moved on to Danny's room. Then the bathroom. Next they went downstairs. Becky, the twins, D.J., and Lee were already waiting in the living room.

Please, let her be down here! Michelle thought.

"Let's divide up again," Becky said. "The boys and I will take the kitchen. The rest of you search in here."

Cassie started checking the couch. Stephanie looked under the rug. Michelle took the cushions off the chairs. D.J. shook out the newspapers and magazines.

They looked for nearly an hour. And they still didn't find Natasha. Michelle didn't know what to do. She was so scared!

"What am I going to tell Dad?" she said. "And Mrs. Wexley and the rest of the kids? They're all going to hate me!" She picked up one of the couch cushions and tossed it down. "Boris is going to hate me too!" she cried. "I've lost his best friend."

"You can't give up yet, Michelle," Cassie said. "Natasha's got to be somewhere. Let's go search in the kitchen. There are lots of places for a mouse to hide in there."

But they didn't find Natasha in the kitchen, either. The whole group trooped back into the living room.

"Think, everybody!" Michelle said. "Where could she be?"

The room grew quiet. Everyone tried to think of a new place to look.

Suddenly they heard someone at the

front door. A key jangled in the lock. The door swung open.

Michelle's heart flipped over. She buried her head under a pillow. It's Dad! she thought. Now he's going to find out about Natasha. And he's going to be really mad!

Chapter 9

Footsteps stopped in front of the couch. Right next to her. Uh-oh, thought Michelle. This is it!

Suddenly someone jerked the pillow off her head. *"BOO!"*

"Eeek!" Michelle squealed, and jumped off the couch.

Everyone laughed, and Michelle opened her eyes. It wasn't her father at all—it was Joey!

"Whew!" Michelle said. She flopped back onto the couch with her hand over her heart. Thank goodness! There was still time to find Natasha before her dad got home.

"Well, well," Joey said. He looked around at the living room. It was a mess! "What do we have here? A rearrange-the-furniture party?"

Michelle just groaned and shook her head.

"It's a hunt-for-Natasha party," Stephanie said. "She's on the loose."

"Natasha, the little white mouse?" Joey said in his Russian accent. "Gee, Michelle . . ."

"I know, Joey," Michelle said. "I'm in big trouble."

"Maybe not," Joey said. He thought a second. "I know. Why don't we set some traps?"

Michelle gasped. "I don't want to kill her! I just want to find her."

"Don't worry," Joey said. "We won't use real mousetraps. We'll just use the bait. See, we put a piece of cheese in every room. We wait awhile. Then we look to see if any of the cheese has been eaten. Then we'll know which room she's in."

"Cool idea," Lee said. "But use peanut butter. Mice really like it. You can put a little blob on a cracker. Not too much, or you won't know if she ate any."

"Good thinking," Joey said. He rubbed his hands together. "Okay, gang. Let's lure out Natasha!"

The group hurried into the kitchen. They smeared crackers with a tiny amount of peanut butter.

Becky and the twins set their bait on the third floor. Michelle, her sisters, and Cassie put theirs on the second. Lee put crackers in the living room and kitchen. Joey took some downstairs.

Then they all met in the living room again. "Now what?" Michelle asked.

"Now we just act normal," Joey said.

He sat in a big chair and stretched out his legs.

Stephanie, D.J., Lee, and Cassie shared the couch. The twins and Becky sat on the rug. Michelle stood in the middle of the room. She was too worried to sit.

For a few seconds nobody said a word. Then Stephanie started laughing. "This isn't normal. This is weird!"

"Shhh!" Michelle said. "Let's be quiet so Natasha won't be scared to come out." She glanced at the peanut butter cracker at the foot of the stairs. "It has to work," she whispered. "It just has to! I bet Natasha's getting hungry."

"Sure," Lee said. "So am I. Do you have any more of those great chocolate chip cookies?"

"How can you eat?" Cassie asked. "Aren't you worried?"

"Yes. But my stomach's not."

"They're in a jar on the kitchen counter," Michelle told Lee. "You can check the cracker in the kitchen while you're in there."

Lee came back munching a cookie. Michelle looked at him hopefully. But he just shook his head.

Suddenly Michelle heard something. "Lee! Is that you?" she asked.

"Is that me what?"

"Chewing?"

"Nope. I'm finished. Why?"

"Shhh!" Michelle held up her hand. "Listen! I hear chewing!"

"You're right," Cassie whispered. "I hear it too. It's coming from upstairs."

"It's awfully loud for a mouse," D.J. said.

"Wait a sec," Joey said. "We shouldn't be able to hear anything. Didn't you close the doors upstairs so Natasha couldn't run from room to room?"

"Uh-oh," Stephanie said. "I didn't think of that."

"Me either!" Michelle said. "Come on. Let's find out what's up there!"

They all raced upstairs. "The whole cracker's gone!" Michelle called out from her room.

"From my room, too!" D.J. yelled.

"I hear something," Stephanie said. She was standing outside Danny's room. She started to go in. But then Comet darted out and raced past her. He had cracker crumbs in his hair. And a little dab of peanut butter on his nose!

"It's Comet!" Michelle cried. "He's eating all our bait! Quick, we've got to catch him. He might find Natasha and eat her, too!"

Everyone headed for the stairs. Comet dashed around the couch. Then he stopped to gobble up the cracker near the coffee table.

"Comet, stop!" Michelle called out. She chased him around the living room. Then she grabbed him around the shoulders and tumbled with him to the floor.

Just then the front door swung open. Michelle pushed her hair out of her face and looked up.

Danny stepped into the living room.

Chapter 10

Comet raced around and sat down behind Danny's legs. Then he peered out at the crowd that had just chased him down the stairs.

Danny smiled. "Hi, everybody. Is this a welcoming committee?"

"Not exactly, Dad," Michelle said. She gulped. "It's a search party."

Danny looked around the living room. The rug was still partly rolled up. Two of the couch pillows were still on the floor. Magazines were scattered all over the table.

"What happened?" Danny asked, looking at each of them. "What's lost?"

Michelle gulped again. She didn't want to tell him. But she had to. "Natasha," she whispered.

Danny laughed. "Gee, Michelle. For a second I thought you said Natasha. Isn't that funny?"

Michelle slowly shook her head. She cleared her throat. "I *did* say Natasha, Dad. She's missing."

"She escaped, Mr. Tanner," Cassie said.

"Escaped?" Danny looked around the room again. "In the house?"

"Yeah," Stephanie said. "We looked all over. And then Joey had this great idea about putting food in all the rooms."

"Peanut butter," Lee added. "On crackers. Mice really like peanut butter."

"Poor Natasha. I just know she's starving," Michelle said. "Now she'll never get any peanut butter. And we'll never find her because Comet ate all the bait."

Danny looked down at Comet. The dog was still hiding behind his legs.

"He's scared because we were chasing him," Michelle explained. "I was afraid he might eat Natasha."

"Why don't I just put him in the back-yard for a while?" Joey said. "Come on, Comet. Want to go out?" He took the dog outside.

"Dad?" Michelle said. "I know I'm in big trouble. But will you promise me something before you yell at me?"

"What's that, honey?"

"Please don't start vacuuming!" Michelle said. She was trying not to cry. "You might suck Natasha up!"

Danny patted her shoulder. "I'm not going to yell. And I promise not to vacuum until we find Natasha."

"But we've looked everywhere, Dad," D.J. said.

"I looked in the potty," Alex said.

Danny smiled. "That was a big help, Alex."

"What should we do now?" Michelle asked.

"We stay on mouse alert," Danny said. "Everybody keep looking. Everywhere."

"Right!" Michelle said. She started for the staircase.

"Not you, Michelle," Danny said. "I'd like to talk to you for a minute first."

Michelle stopped walking. This is it, she thought. Now I'm going to get a lecture. I'll probably get grounded. Probably for a year. And I'll never, ever get my own pet.

"I think it's time for me to go home," Lee said.

"Me too." Cassie smiled at Michelle. "Don't worry. I just know you're going to find Natasha. Call me when you do, okay?"

"Okay. Thanks for helping me look," Michelle said to her friends. She walked them to the door and waved good-bye.

Then Michelle sat down on the couch with her father.

Danny didn't yell. But he used his most serious voice. "I think we should talk about the *R* word," he said.

Michelle stared at the rug. "Responsibility?" she whispered.

"That's right."

"Okay." Michelle took a deep breath. "It's all my fault!" she said. "I was in a hurry to go to the carnival. I didn't close the cage door tight enough. I was getting bored with the mice. I should have read about them, like Lee did. I didn't even know they could climb out of their cage. Or jump through hoops!"

Danny looked surprised. "Mice can jump through hoops?"

Michelle nodded. "But not Natasha, because she's gone and it's my fault! Now Mrs. Wexley's going to hate me. And so will all the kids at school. You too, Dad. And now I'll never get my own pet!"

"I'll never hate you, Michelle." Danny put his arm around her. "Honey, you made a mistake. You were careless. Everybody is sometimes. The trick is to try hard not to make the same mistake twice."

"I think I can learn real fast, Dad," Michelle said.

"I'm sure you can." Danny hugged Michelle. And Michelle felt a little better. But she was still worried about Natasha.

An hour later the family gathered for dinner. They still hadn't found the mouse. It was one of the quietest dinners in the history of the Tanner house.

Michelle couldn't eat. She kept thinking about going to school the next day without Natasha. How would she ever explain what happened to Mrs. Wexley and the other kids? It was going to be awful!

After dinner Michelle kept looking. But secretly she thought it was hopeless. Natasha was gone. Or else she'd been eaten by Comet.

Michelle tried hard not to cry. Crying wouldn't bring Natasha back. But her eyes kept filling up with tears.

She was about to check the couch cushions for the third time. But just then Jesse came home from the concert in the park. He'd been gone since early that morning.

"Hey, Michelle," he said. "How's it going?"

"Hi, Uncle Jesse." Michelle sniffed and picked up another cushion.

Jesse set his guitar case on the coffee table. "Looking for something?"

Michelle dropped the cushion and burst into tears.

Becky and the twins came downstairs. Danny and Comet came in from the kitchen. Michelle kept crying.

"Michelle, honey, what did I say?" Jesse asked.

"What *did* you say?" Becky asked.

"I asked her if she was looking for something."

Michelle cried harder.

"Tasha," Alex said.

"She's gone," Nicky said.

"And it's all my fault!" Michelle cried.

"Gee, Michelle, I'm sorry." Jesse patted her on the back. "Listen, maybe we could just go to the pet store and buy another one."

"It wouldn't be Natasha," Michelle said. "Besides, that would be cheating."

"Yeah, you're right," Jesse said. "That was a lousy idea."

Michelle wiped her eyes and pulled another cushion off the couch.

"How was the concert?" Becky asked Jesse.

"It was fantastic!" Jesse said. "There were hundreds of people there. They really loved the band."

Nicky and Alex opened the guitar case

while their parents talked. Alex started to pull out the guitar.

"Careful," Jesse said. "Here. Let me help you." He carefully lifted out the guitar and put it on the floor. Alex started to pick at the strings. Nicky explored the guitar case.

"Everybody was playing old rock-and-roll music," Jesse went on. "I even did one of my Elvis songs."

"Tasha," Nicky said softly.

"I know, Nicky," Michelle told him. "I miss her too."

"Tasha," Nicky said, more loudly.

"Nicky, you're making Michelle feel bad," Becky said. "Besides, Natasha doesn't come when you call, honey."

"Tasha!" Nicky shouted. He grabbed Michelle's hand and pointed at the guitar case.

Michelle looked down into the case. There was one big space for the guitar. But there were also several little compartments in it. One of them held packages of extra strings. Another one held a bunch of guitar picks.

Nicky lifted the lid on the third one and laughed.

Michelle gasped. She couldn't believe her eyes.

Inside was a tiny white mouse.

Chapter 11

"Natasha!" Michelle squealed. "It's Natasha!"

Danny peered into the case. Then he breathed a sigh of relief. "It sure is."

"Hey, everybody!" Michelle shouted. "Nicky found Natasha!"

D.J. and Stephanie came running downstairs. Joey raced up from the basement.

"Where was she?" Stephanie asked.

"In my guitar case," Jesse said. "But I don't understand how . . . Oh, I know! I left my case in the hall this morning when I came back from rehearsal. I guess it wasn't closed all the way. Natasha must have climbed in." He laughed. "How do you like that? Natasha went to a rock concert!"

Michelle picked up the mouse and rubbed her on the head. "Natasha, I was so worried!" she said. "I thought Comet had eaten you. I'm going to put you back with Boris right now."

Michelle ran upstairs and put Natasha in the mouse house with Boris. This time she made sure the cage door was closed tight.

Then Michelle went back downstairs. She told Joey it was okay to bring Comet back in from the yard. Comet looked as if he was afraid everyone would start chasing him again. He went behind a big chair and tried to stay out of sight.

"Well, the great mouse hunt is over," Stephanie said. "It looks like you're not in trouble after all, Michelle."

Michelle knew everything would be okay with Mrs. Wexley and the rest of the kids. But she still didn't feel right. "Dad?" she said.

"Yes, Michelle?"

"I know I messed up, and I'm sorry," she said. "But I've learned. I really have. And I still want my own pet."

Danny looked serious. "Well, honey . . ."

"But not yet," Michelle said. "It's a big job being responsible for a pet all by yourself. I want to practice some more."

"Not with more mice!" D.J. cried out.

Michelle shook her head. "I'm going to practice being as responsible as I can with the pet we already have."

"With Comet, you mean?" Danny said. "That's a good idea, Michelle. I'm proud of you."

"Thanks, Dad," Michelle said. "And at least I know I won't lose Comet." She pointed to the chair. The dog's golden tail was sticking out from behind it. "Comet's way too big to hide!"

For information about
Mary-Kate + Ashley's Fun Club™,
the Olsen Twins' only
official fan club, write to:

Mary-Kate + Ashley's Fun Club™
859 Hollywood Way, Suite 412
Burbank, California 91505

FULL HOUSE™
Michelle

#1: THE GREAT PET PROJECT

#2: THE SUPER-DUPER SLEEPOVER PARTY

#3: MY TWO BEST FRIENDS

#4: LUCKY, LUCKY DAY

#5: THE GHOST IN MY CLOSET

#6: BALLET SURPRISE

Available from

Published by Pocket Books

™ & © 1994, 1995 Warner Bros. Television All Rights Reserved. 1033-09

A series of novels based on your favorite character from the hit TV show!

FULL HOUSE™
Stephanie

PHONE CALL FROM A FLAMINGO THE
BOY-OH-BOY NEXT DOOR
TWIN TROUBLES
HIP HOP TILL YOU DROP
HERE COMES THE BRAND NEW ME
THE SECRET'S OUT
DADDY'S NOT-SO-LITTLE GIRL
P.S. FRIENDS FOREVER
GETTING EVEN WITH
THE FLAMINGOES
THE DUDE OF MY DREAMS
BACK-TO-SCHOOL COOL
PICTURE ME FAMOUS
TWO-FOR-ONE CHRISTMAS FUN

Available from Minstrel® Books
Published by Pocket Books

™ & © 1993, 1994, 1995 Warner Bros. Television. All Rights Reserved. 929-10

Join the gang—and spend sixteen months with your favorite characters from the hit TV show FULL HOUSE!

FULL HOUSE™

1995-1996 CALENDAR

D.J., Stephanie, Michelle, Uncle Jesse—even Comet—are all here in your very own calendar to get you through the school year and beyond!

Filled with photos from all eight seasons of the hit sitcom, this calendar has plenty of room for you to add your own important dates! Keep track of birthdays, parties, and family gatherings while you watch your favorite characters grow-up over the years!

From Minstrel® Books

Published by Pocket Books

™ & © 1995 Warner Bros. Television

1096-01